The Lonely Whale

By Ben Morris
Illustrated by Alex Tawns

For Gwil on his
fourth birthday
Best wishes
Ben

Ben
For Faelen, with all my love.

Alex
To our family - the ones we came with, and the ones we made along the way.

This is 52, the very lonely whale.

Most whales travel the world in herds.
Most whales travel in a family.
But 52 doesn't have a herd.
52 doesn't have anybody.

Most whales sing in a special song that all others know.

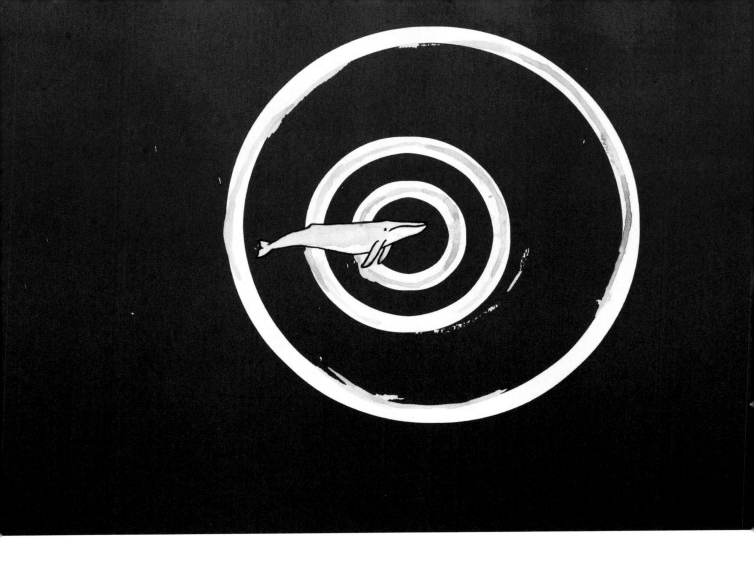

52 doesn't know that song.
52 only has his own song.

52 searches the ocean for his song.
52 searches the ocean for a herd.
52 searches the ocean for a family.

Suddenly 52 hears a new song.
A song a little like his own, coming from the reef.

To find his herd 52 swims faster than any whale can swim ...

But it wasn't a herd. It was Joe, the guitar playing
turtle!
Joe is also a kind turtle and hearing 52's tale of
loneliness he decides to help him find him his herd.

A little later Joe and 52 hear a new song.
A song a little like 52's own, coming from the surface.

To find 52's herd they jump higher than any whale, or turtle
can jump ...

But it wasn't his herd. It was Becky, the trumpet playing
seagull!
Becky is also a caring seagull and hearing 52's tale of
loneliness she decides to help 52 find his herd.

A little later 52, Joe, and Becky hear a new song.
A song a little like 52's own, coming from the deep.

To find 52's herd they swim deeper than any whale, turtle, or
seagull can swim ...

But it wasn't 52's herd. It was Chip the drumming Giant
Squid!
Chip is also a lovely Giant squid and hearing 52's tale of
loneliness he decides to help 52 find his herd.

A little later 52, Joe, Becky and Chip hear a new song.
A song a little like 52's own, coming from far away.

To find 52's herd they swim further than any whale, turtle,
seagull, or Giant Squid can swim ...

But it wasn't 52's herd. It was Sarah, the double-bass playing orca!

Sarah is also a compassionate orca and hearing 52's tale of loneliness she decides to help 52 find his herd.

And so they search and search all over the ocean,
but poor 52 cannot find a song like his own.

Poor 52 cannot find a herd.
Poor 52 cannot find a family.

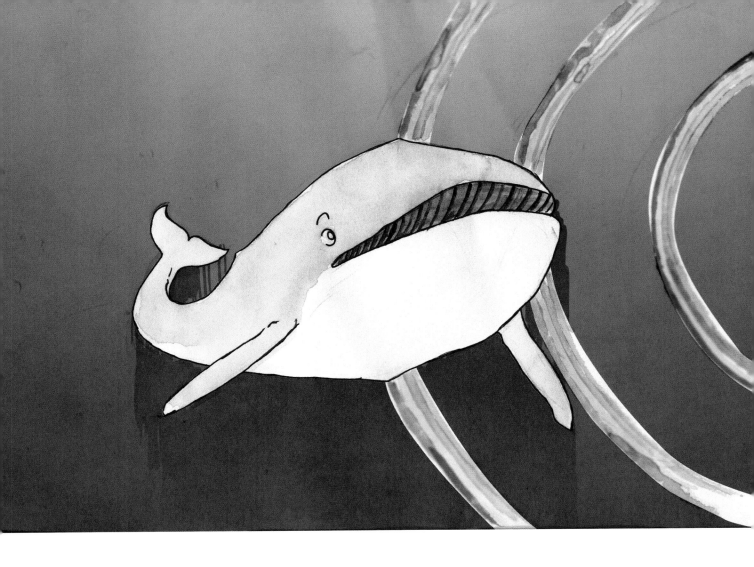

Until one day 52 hears a song a lot like his own.
But where is his herd?
Where is his family?

It's his friends!

Because there might be nobody like 52,
but he has found friends.
And he has made his own herd.
And he has made his own family.
And he will never be lonely again.

And they became the best band ever!

The End.

The story of 52 is inspired by a real whale who "sings" at 52Hz and was first recorded in 1989. Nobody knows why this whale sings at a much higher pitch than other whales (the blue whale sings at 10-40Hz). Some think he may be a hybrid of a blue whale and another species, others have suggested he may be deaf. He was last heard in 2004 so we may never know (though we have been informed he is working on his new album).

This book was designed to make reading as easy as possible for children with reading difficulties and follows the Dyslexia Style Guide produced by the British Dyslexia Association as far as possible.
The font used is Open Dyslexic, a free font designed to increase readability. It can be found at http://opendyslexic.org/

If you have any suggestions, please email us at lonelywhalestory@gmail.com and we will be happy to make what changes we can to the book.

Printed in Great Britain
by Amazon